MY TEDDY BEAR

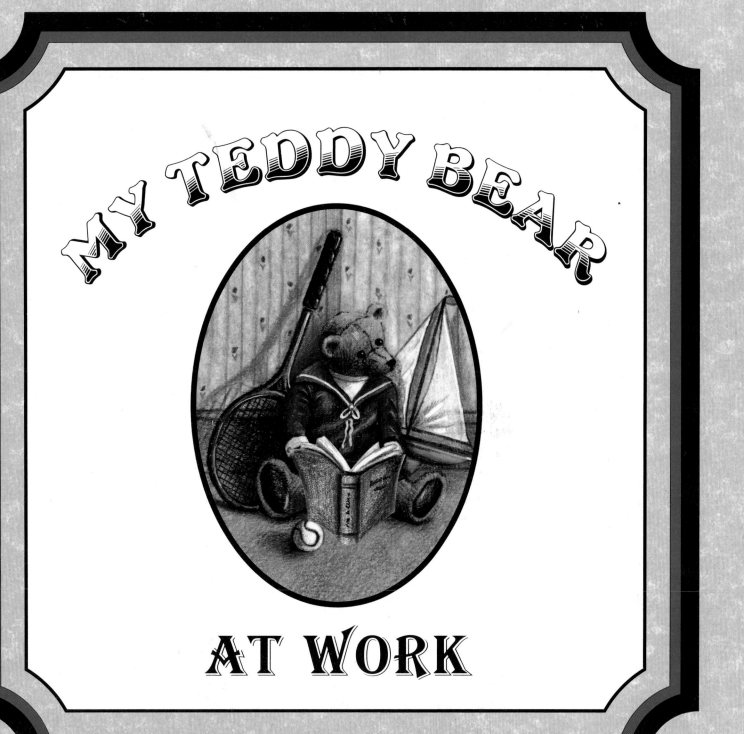

AT WORK

Teddy Bear and Clown are reading a newspaper. Clown has found a story about a fireman. There is a picture of him in uniform standing next to his fire engine. Clown would like to be a fireman too. Teddy makes a list of all his favourite jobs. 'I will just have to try them all,' he says.

Teddy would like to work in an office. He could write important letters on a typewriter. There is a lot to do, sticking stamps on envelopes, and then sealing them up for the post. He is much too busy to keep his desk tidy. Teddy is a messy worker.

'Perhaps I would make a good doctor,' says Teddy. He wears a special white coat, and carries a funny instrument called a stethoscope. Teddy gets lots of practice bandaging Wooden Doll's hand. He has already put Toy Soldier's arm in a sling after he was hurt in a make-believe battle!

This is Teddy Bear's shop. He has a pair of

scales to weigh fruit and vegetables. Rag Doll

is buying some of the fruit that Teddy has just

weighed. She wants an apple and a banana

for her lunch. Teddy will put them in a bag

while Rag Doll finds two coins, one for each

kind of fruit.

Teddy Bear likes to play the piano. He is giving a concert to some of his friends. He looks very smart in his white tie, and black tail-coat. His friend Toy Soldier plays a musical instrument too. He beats his drum in time to the music.

Now Teddy is a circus star. Rag Rabbit and Clown are pretending to be his 'lions'. He has borrowed Rag Doll's whip and top so that he can make a cracking noise just like they used to do in the circus. Teddy likes wearing the shining uniform, with its brass buttons and hat.

Being a teacher is fun. Teddy Bear draws on a blackboard. He is showing the toys how to do their sums. They are learning how to add up. Rag Doll thinks the sum is very easy, and she has already finished. The others are finding it much harder. They haven't finished.

Teddy Bear has made his blackboard into an easel, so that he can paint a picture. An artist mixes paints together, and sloshes them onto paper. Teddy likes being an artist because it is a messy job. He likes to paint, and today he has painted a picture of himself in the garden.

Trying all these different jobs is hungry work for a little bear, so Teddy decides he'd like to be a chef. He wears a tall white hat and an apron. Teddy is going to make vegetable soup, but he isn't a very good cook. He doesn't realise that he has to cut the vegetables up before they go into the pan!

Now Teddy Bear has tried all the jobs he listed

in his notebook. He is really not sure which

job he likes best. Wooden Doll has brought

Teddy his favourite meal, a glass of milk and

bread with strawberry jam. 'Perhaps I will just

be a stay-at-home bear,' he says,

sipping his milk.